Construction Vehicles at Work

Concrete Mixers

by Kathryn Clay

CAPSTONE PRESS
a capstone imprint

Little Pebble is published by Capstone Press,
1710 Roe Crest Drive, North Mankato, Minnesota 56003
www.mycapstone.com

Library of Congress Cataloging-in-Publication Data
Cataloging-in-publication information is on file with the Library of Congress.
ISBN 978-1-5157-8016-8 (library binding)
ISBN 978-1-5157-8018-2 (paperback)
ISBN 978-1-5157-8020-5 (eBook PDF)

Editorial Credits
Shelly Lyons, editor; Juliette Peters, designer;
Wanda Winch, media researcher; Laura Manthe, production specialist

Photo Credits
Alamy: Randy Duchaine, 17; iStockphoto: ewg3D, 7, JodiJacobson, 15; Shutterstock: Art Konovalov, 9, Blanscape, cover, Janos Huszka, metal plate and stripe design, KPG_Payless, 11, Mark Atkins, 5, Natykach Nataliia, 3, Pablo Rogat, 1, Pablos33, concrete texture, Paul Vasarhelyi, 19, Stefano Ember, 13, Verena Matthew, 21, Yuliyan Velchev, metal texture

Printed in China.
010290F17

Table of Contents

About Concrete Mixers

Look!

Here comes a concrete mixer.

This truck is tough.

It hauls a heavy load.

Dane drives.

He sits in the cab.

cab

See the drum?

It spins.

drum

The drum has a blade.

It stirs water and sand.

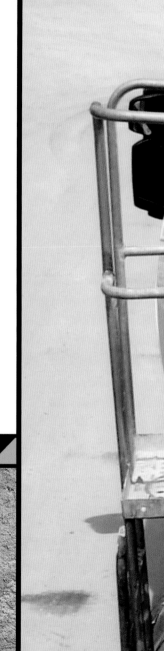

blade

Now the drum spins
the other way.
Then the blade pushes
out the mix.

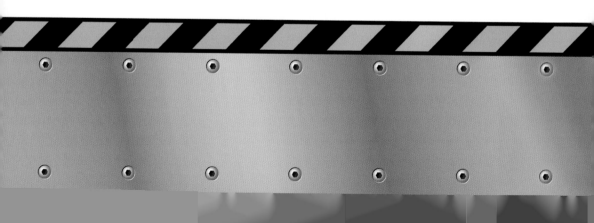

mix

Here is a slide
called the chute.
It is on the back
of the truck.

chute

17

At Work

Len holds the chute.

The wet mix falls out.

It will make a wall.

The wall is done.

Nice job!

Glossary

blade—a wide, curved piece of metal; the blade mixes and pushes out concrete

cab—the place where the driver sits

chute—a slide for moving things down

concrete—a material made from stone or gravel, sand, and water that hardens when dry

drum—a turning container that mixes concrete

haul—to pull or carry a load

mix—a blend

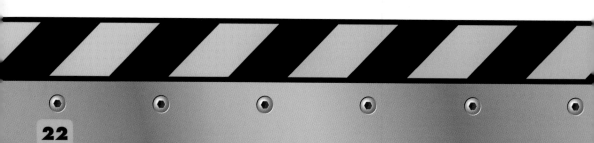

Read More

Graubart, Norman D. *Cement Mixers.* Giants on the Road. New York: PowerKids Press, 2015.

Meister, Cari. *Concrete Mixers.* Machines at Work. Minneapolis: Bullfrog Books, 2017.

Schuh, Mari C. *Community Helpers at the Construction Site.* Community Helpers. North Mankato, Minn.: Capstone Press, 2017.

Internet Sites

FactHound offers a safe, fun way to find Internet sites related to this book. All of the sites on FactHound have been researched by our staff.

Here's all you do:
Visit *www.facthound.com*
Type in this code: 9781515780168

Check out projects, games and lots more at
www.capstonekids.com

Index